PAULI MURRAY

SHOUTING for the RIGHTS of ALL PEOPLE

DEBORAH NELSON LINCK
Illustrations by ANGELA CORBIN

Morehouse Publishing
NEW YORK

Morehouse Publishing, 19 East 34th Street, New York, NY 10016
Morehouse Publishing is an imprint of Church Publishing Incorporated.

Cover art by Angela Corbin
Cover design by Jennifer Kopec, 2Pug Design
Typeset by Rose Design

Library of Congress Cataloging-in-Publication Data

Names: Nelson Linck, Deborah, author. | Corbin, Angela, 1973- illustrator.
Title: Pauli Murray : shouting for the rights of all people / Deborah
   Nelson Linck ; illustrated by Angela Corbin.
Description: New York, NY : Morehouse Publishing, [2022] | Audience: Ages
   6-12 | Audience: Grades 4-6
Identifiers: LCCN 2021059494 (print) | LCCN 2021059495 (ebook) |
   ISBN 9781640655577 (paperback) | ISBN 9781640655584 (epub)
Subjects: LCSH: Murray, Pauli, 1910-1985--Juvenile literature. | African
   Americans--Biography--Juvenile literature. | African American civil
   rights workers--Biography--Juvenile literature. | African American
   women--Biography--Juvenile literature. | African American women civil
   rights workers--Biography--Juvenile literature.
Classification: LCC E185.97.M95 N45 2022 (print) | LCC E185.97.M95
   (ebook) | DDC 305.89/96073--dc23/eng/20220131

LC record available at https://lccn.loc.gov/2021059494
LC ebook record available at https://lccn.loc.gov/2021059495

This book is dedicated to all those "fearfully and wonderfully made" individuals that continue to inspire my life.

Special thanks to all the people who have laid eyes on, edited, and helped me birth this book.

To Van, Ja'Lon, Deb, Rob, Peter, Sarah, James, Lisa, Andrew, Alex, Wendy, Nancy, Maggie, and Dan, thank you for your love and support.

Contents

The Use of Pronouns
in This Book

I have given a lot of thought to pronoun usage in this book. It is important to note that Pauli Murray used singular "she"/"her" pronouns during her life. The use of more inclusive language has its own history, and it continues to evolve. Today many choose to use gender-neutral pronouns, such as "they" and "their." Had Pauli lived at a different time "she" might have selected pronouns that more accurately reflected "her" gender identity. For this reason I have chosen to use a combination of pronouns to both respect Pauli's voice and honor their identity.

A Note to the Reader

Welcome—

I'm so excited that you have chosen to learn about the amazing life of Pauli Murray. You may not have heard of Pauli before, but I hope that when you finish this book you will want to share Pauli's story with others. It might help in reading this story to know a little about the world in which Pauli grew up.

Anna Pauline Murray was born more than one hundred years ago. In the early 1900s, clothing, transportation, and schools looked different. People's differences were not celebrated. Instead, fear and lack of understanding led people to form prejudices and create unfair laws based on race, gender, and even who a person loved. Two examples that made life difficult during this time were segregation and Jim Crow laws. Segregation meant separating people by their skin color or race. Black Americans and white Americans had separate communities where they lived. Restaurants, schools, movie theaters, and swimming pools were all segregated. Water fountains, restrooms, and buses were separated and labeled with one place for African American customers and the other for white American customers.

Jim Crow laws were named after an awkward enslaved character in a popular musical show around 1830. These laws made segregation legal for about one hundred years. Jim Crow laws were strictly enforced using fear, the threat of paying large fines, jail time, and harsh, violent treatment. These unfair laws divided Americans in towns and cities across the country. Treatment that discriminated against African Americans became a way of life. Living freely and achieving their dreams was a great challenge.

It was also the case during Pauli's life that women were not treated fairly or as equals. There were jobs women were expected to do and other jobs they were not. Women's voices were ignored. They could not vote, they could not attend some schools, have leadership roles, or earn as much money as men. Women were expected to wear dresses, skirts, and suits. Pauli named the unfair treatment "Jane Crow." The combination of Pauli's race and gender made life twice as hard because of Jim Crow and Jane Crow laws and expectations.

Pauli Murray lived until the year 1985 and dedicated her life to creating change. At the age of seventy-four, Pauli lived long enough to see many of these laws and ways of life changed for both African Americans and women. Pauli Murray fought for equality and freedom using great intelligence, brilliant writing skills, a handy typewriter, and a strong voice to speak out against unfair treatment of all people.

Maybe after reading about Pauli Murray, you'll be inspired to dream about how you will use your gifts and talents to change our world.

Happy Reading!

1 ▪ The Beginning

Swirling around us at birth are all the possibilities for what and who we can be. Parents and family hold hopes and dreams for their newborns, anxiously awaiting the gifts they will bring into the world. From the time we are born, we are chosen to be special, unique, and awesome, made in our Creator's image. There is a religious verse, or psalm, that describes this as being "fearfully and wonderfully made." This was all true for Anna Pauline. Full of hope and possibilities, Anna Pauline grew into a truly special person who shared her gifts, shouting for the rights of all people and changing the world.

On November 20, 1910, the world welcomed Anna Pauline Murray. Born in Baltimore, Maryland, she was the child of William Murray and Agnes Fitzgerald. Her father was a public schoolteacher and her mother a nurse. Anna Pauline was the fourth of the six Murray children. The oldest sibling, Grace, was followed by Mildred, Willie, Anna Pauline, Rosetta, and the youngest, Robert Fitzgerald.

Anna Pauline's life was like a winding path that unfolded before her. The journey had many twists and turns and often was not easy. There were challenges, things that would try to block her path. Helping her along the way were family members, friends, and a number of mentors that would gently guide her throughout her life and keep her focused and moving forward. These guardians would faithfully hold the vision for Anna Pauline that she was indeed someone special.

Sadly, Anna Pauline's mother died when Anna Pauline was only three and a half years old. After her mother's death, Anna Pauline's father was unable to care for the children and sent them to live with relatives. Grace, Mildred, Will, and Rosetta went to live with family members in Baltimore. Anna Pauline moved to Durham, North Carolina, to live with her grandparents—her mother's parents—Robert and Cornelia Fitzgerald, and two aunts, Sallie and Pauline. When Anna Pauline was thirteen, a short nine years after her mother's death, her father was killed.

Anna Pauline was the only child in her grandparents' home. Some of her earliest memories were of being held and rocked by her grandmother. Anna Pauline felt safe and loved, and she always held a special place in her heart for her grandmother. Anna Pauline's parents were kept alive in her memory through stories her aunts and grandparents would tell. There were family pictures on the walls in their home and she was allowed

to ask endless questions about them. The stories, lovingly told, along with the pictures helped Anna Pauline to know, love, and appreciate her parents.

Anna Pauline shared the same name with her Aunt Pauline. Many times, children are named for a relative who is well loved. Aunt Pauline was her mother's oldest sister and the two sisters had been very fond of each other. Her aunt soon became like a mother to Anna Pauline and later adopted her.

Aunt Pauline was a no-nonsense person. She did not smile often, but Anna Pauline felt loved. Her aunt was firm, yet kind. She had expectations and encouraged Anna Pauline to always work toward her best. Aunt Pauline also helped Anna Pauline see that life had many choices, helping her to understand that choices have consequences, good and bad. Anna Pauline sometimes found out the hard way when she made poor choices and Aunt Pauline did not come to the rescue. Aunt Pauline helped Anna Pauline face difficult choices throughout her life.

2 · Faith

Faith was at the center of family life for Anna Pauline. There was a wooden cross over the mantlepiece in her grandparent's home, a place of honor. Many evenings Anna Pauline would read the Bible to her grandmother. At the age of nine, Anna Pauline was confirmed in the Episcopal Church by Bishop Henry B. Delany, a family friend. He was one of the first two African American bishops in the Episcopal Church. Many years later, Anna Pauline visited Bishop Delaney when he was very ill. She and her aunt said final prayers with the bishop. He called Anna Pauline to his bedside and spoke words that would never be forgotten. Almost as if he were looking into the future, Bishop Delaney said, "You are a child of destiny." Aunt Pauline would hold this vision and remind Anna Pauline of it often.

Anna Pauline continued to honor familiar faith traditions throughout her life. As a youngster, Anna Pauline regularly attended church with Aunt Pauline each Sunday. As a young adult and into adulthood, Anna Pauline continued to attend and participate in the work of the church. Anna Pauline did not always agree with the church but always returned to the familiar faith-centered life of her youth.

3 ▪ Childhood

Anna Pauline had a very active childhood and kept busy with school, chores, and family gatherings. As a member of the household, everyone was expected to help with housework. Even young children worked—there was no allowance in those days. Anna Pauline stacked wood used to warm the house, filled oil lamps (the home didn't have electricity), scrubbed the outhouse (the outdoor bathroom), and worked in the garden. Anna Pauline read to her grandparents and ran errands for relatives. Often, Anna Pauline acted as messenger between households because there was no telephone.

It's hard to imagine but at age eight Anna Pauline already had a paying job. After completing her Saturday chores around the house, young Anna Pauline was allowed to walk across town, about a mile. By this time her Aunt Sallie had married and moved into her own home. Anna Pauline would help Aunt Sallie with household chores. After finishing the work, she was paid twenty-five cents.

At age ten, Anna Pauline sold magazine subscriptions and took on a Saturday afternoon paper route. A paper route is a job delivering newspapers to the same houses each day. The paper route job lasted until she was in high school. With the money saved, she bought skates, a bike, and even a high school class ring.

4 ▪ School

West End Public was the elementary school for Black students in first through sixth grades. It was a large, old, two-story building. The paint was peeling on the outside, the wooden floors were rough, and the bathrooms leaked. The water fountains did not work and the dirt playground had no swings and no trees for shade. Books for students at West End were old, used, and torn.

On the way to school, Anna Pauline passed students going to the elementary school for white children. Their school was brick with a nice lawn. A fence surrounded the school and there were swings on the playground. It was clear the schools were not equal. Anna Pauline and her schoolmates could see and feel the difference between the two schools.

Aunt Pauline was a well-respected first grade teacher at West End Public School. Anna Pauline began to attend school with her aunt at age four. There was no preschool or kindergarten, so she sat in Aunt Pauline's classroom every day. Unable to participate, Anna Pauline sat quietly, taking in all the information the other students were learning. By the end of the school year, Anna Pauline surprised her aunt by reading aloud!

Once enrolled in school, Anna Pauline worked hard, was smart, and loved reading and learning new things. Anna Pauline was an "A" student. There were still challenges for this bright student: Anna Pauline was talkative, liked to pass notes, annoyed classmates, and encouraged them to misbehave. Anna Pauline was full of energy that just seemed to bubble out of her. This mischievous behavior caused Anna Pauline to have poor grades in school conduct.

Anna Pauline felt that she was different from other students at school, sometimes feeling sad and left out when other students talked about their parents or brothers and sisters. Her five siblings were miles away, and they did not visit one another often. Her parents were alive in her heart through stories and pictures, but it was not the same as having them alive in their home.

Another difference was that Anna Pauline was left-handed. This is not a problem for children today, but when Anna Pauline was young it was thought to be wrong and backward if a child used their left hand for writing. Many people would force children to learn to write with their right hand instead. Anna Pauline was smart and learned to write with both hands.

The elementary grades passed quickly, and soon Anna Pauline entered Hillside High School, the first high school for African Americans in Durham. Most days, Anna Pauline walked to school, about three miles each way. Hillside High was a new school made of red brick with its own library, cafeteria, and auditorium. Students attending Hillside only received an education through grade eleven. Twenty-seven years after it opened, Hillside High School would add twelfth grade. This created a problem for graduating students who wanted to attend college, as they would not have enough credits. This would later be an obstacle for Anna Pauline even though she graduated at the top of the class.

In high school Anna Pauline outgrew much of the disruptive behavior of her younger days, playing basketball, participating on the debate team, helping to edit the school newspaper, and taking piano lessons alongside regular classwork. She also kept the paper route.

In tenth grade Anna Pauline took a special class to learn typing, bookkeeping, and shorthand, all good skills for becoming a secretary. These skills came in handy upon entering college and in several jobs after college.

After four years of hard work both in and out of school, Anna Pauline graduated at the top of the high school class and received a scholarship to attend Wilberforce College in Ohio. Wilberforce was a college for Black students. It was the first college owned by Black Americans in the United States. Wilberforce was a fine school, but Anna Pauline knew it was a segregated school and wanted something different. While she admired many of the high school teachers who had attended there, Anna Pauline's heart was set on attending Columbia University in New York City. In New York, she dreamed of escaping the Jim Crow laws of Durham. Anna Pauline did not accept the scholarship to Wilberforce.

At the age of fifteen, Anna Pauline and Aunt Pauline visited a cousin in New York to explore colleges. Once in New York, there were several disappointments. First, they discovered Columbia University did not accept women. Anna Pauline and Aunt Pauline tried a women's college near Columbia, but they did not have enough money for Anna Pauline to attend.

Their final attempt to be admitted to school was Hunter College, a public university in New York City. To attend, Anna Pauline would need to live in New York and to pass several high school courses not available at Hillside High School in Durham. These courses could take up to two years to complete.

To overcome these obstacles, Anna Pauline moved in with her cousin and enrolled in Richmond Hill High School. Richmond Hill High School is in Queens, New York. While New York was almost 500 miles from Durham, North Carolina, it seemed even farther away in other ways. Richmond Hill High was integrated. African American students and white students attended the same school. This was a new experience for Anna Pauline as the only African American student in the

class. With great determination, hard work, and the guidance
and encouragement of teachers, she completed the course work.
Anna Pauline not only graduated with honors but finished in
just one year. After graduation, Anna Pauline returned home to
work for a year.

5 ▪ Race and Jim Crow Laws

During Anna Pauline's early years, family members and adults often talked about race. Older relatives who were born enslaved were at family gatherings. They shared stories of how they had made lives for themselves after gaining their freedom. Some African Americans were made to feel ashamed of their race. This was not true for Anna Pauline. Learning at home how African Americans had helped build the country, how they were hard workers, owned businesses, fought in wars, became doctors, lawyers, teachers, and important members of their communities gave Anna Pauline a sense of pride. Surrounded by photographs of relatives proudly displayed on the walls, magazines from African American organizations, and books on the shelves by African American authors, Anna Pauline grew up feeling important and as smart as anyone else.

The community around Anna Pauline believed the opposite. Outside the family and close community, white Americans believed that African Americans were not smart, that they were lazy, and that they could only do certain, limited jobs. Sadly, they believed that African Americans and white Americans should not live, work, or play together. They wrote laws that separated people by race. It affected daily life in Durham where Anna Pauline lived. While unfair to African Americans, Jim Crow laws affected white Americans also. Jim Crow laws enforced where you could live, who you could work with, and who your friends could be. It allowed white Americans to feel they were better than African Americans. Growing up with Jim Crow laws, white Americans felt safe. They had not known life any other way. African Americans felt unsafe and lived with fear. They knew their lives mattered and they were not less than anyone. The unfair laws, however, did not protect them.

Living under Jim Crow was exhausting, like carrying an invisible, heavy weight on your shoulders. Anna Pauline found ways around the heaviness. To show disagreement with Jim Crow laws, Anna Pauline made her own personal protests, walking for miles to most places to avoid segregated buses or refusing to attend segregated movie theaters. These unfair laws planted a seed in Anna Pauline's head. After graduation from high school, she would leave Durham, segregation, and

Jim Crow. Instead of unfair laws telling her who she was and what she could and could not do, Anna Pauline would tell the world who she was.

6 ▪ Life as a Young Adult

Anna Pauline's experiences during childhood laid a strong foundation for the person she would become, learning from extended family a sense of belonging, racial pride, and a life centered around faith. Aunt Pauline was a role model, a dedicated teacher, and a respected member of the community. She set expectations for young Anna Pauline and taught her independence and decision making. Throughout her life, Aunt Pauline supported and loved Anna Pauline unconditionally. Anna Pauline worked hard from an early age. Through many jobs, she learned to reach goals through hard work. Living under unfair Jim Crow laws helped her to see and feel life differently. All this offered a foundation for Anna Pauline's life.

In 1928, Anna Pauline began school at Hunter College in New York City. She had grown up in a home where women were taught and encouraged to be independent. She was surrounded by strong women who spoke up for themselves. Growing up, Anna Pauline made her own personal decisions and worked to make money that allowed independence. Hunter

College was an all-female school. While attending there, she learned from women who were in leadership roles and observed women who spoke out for the rights of all women.

As a college student, Anna Pauline felt the independence of being a young adult away from home and challenged popular gender norms of how women "should" look. Women wore skirts and dresses. She occasionally enjoyed wearing pants and preferred short hair. Anna Pauline shortened her name to Pauli and shared their newfound freedom and identity with close friends. Pauli blossomed and began to show the world the special, unique person they were.

During the first year at Hunter, Pauli explored New York City on bicycle, taking in all the sights of the big city. Pauli attended concerts at the Apollo Theater, a famous music hall in Harlem, part of New York City. The theater featured popular African American performers.

Pauli worked many different jobs while in college, which were not always easy to find. Again, they were faced with unfair Jim Crow laws. Want ads in the paper were looking only for white workers. At this time in the United States, banks failed, businesses closed, and many Americans lost their jobs. This was called the Great Depression. Between paying for rent, food, and school, Pauli was poor and often went hungry.

Even with these hardships, college connected Pauli with close friends. Fearlessly, Pauli and one of those friends hitchhiked from New York City to Nebraska and back—1,356 miles! Pauli was surrounded by women of different ages who were smart, independent, professional, and leaders. These women were new role models, and Pauli too was becoming a strong gifted leader.

7 ▪ After College

At Hunter College, Pauli set her sights on becoming a writer. It had long been a dream of theirs. With hard work and a professor who took an interest in their writing, Pauli graduated with a degree in English Literature. This was the first of many successes.

After college, Pauli spent time writing poetry, often using poetry as a way to protest or to express feelings. Pauli wrote about race, life, friendship, and their view of America and the world as they saw it. Their writing inspired, challenged, and offered hope to people who shared the same feelings. Some of Pauli Murray's poems were later published as a book called *Dark Testament and Other Poems*.

Pauli used their writing skills to speak out against unfair laws and practices, learning from a good friend to write letters to people in authority when they disagreed with them. Once, Pauli wrote a letter to the president of the United States, Franklin Roosevelt, disagreeing strongly with a speech he had given. The president did not respond, but the letter was shared with his wife, Eleanor Roosevelt. She took time to answer the letter. Pauli admired Mrs. Roosevelt and continued writing to her when Pauli disagreed with events or practices. Mrs. Roosevelt and Pauli grew up very differently from one another and were different ages, but they soon found common interests and connections. They both agreed in strong leadership roles for women. Mrs. Roosevelt and Pauli learned from one another over the years. The two women exchanged friendly letters and cards. They enjoyed one another's company. Mrs. Roosevelt often invited Pauli to her home for visits. This was a special honor for Pauli. Their respect for one another grew into a lifelong friendship.

Many years and many jobs later, Pauli returned to Durham with a plan. Moving home, they could continue their education while caring for their aunts, who were getting older. In 1938 Pauli applied to the University of North Carolina at Chapel Hill for graduate school. The application was turned down because of their race. The university did not accept African American students. Once again, Pauli faced Jim Crow laws. Pauli spoke out against this unfair practice and challenged the school. Pauli knew they were speaking out not only as an individual but for those students who had come before and had not been admitted. They used their brave voice also to speak for the African American students who would come after. Pauli was never admitted to the university, but did not view this as a defeat. The fight for justice and change by challenging Jim Crow laws was a win for everyone. So, Pauli kept shouting for the rights of all people. Thirteen years later, in 1951, the first Black students were admitted to the university.

Pauli continued to protest unjust laws. In 1940, Pauli and a friend named Adelene McBean were returning home to Durham on a bus. When asked to move to a rear seat, they refused. The two tried to explain why they refused. It did not matter to the bus driver that the seat was broken.

While it seemed unfair, Jim Crow laws like this one were legal and enforced during this time. Pauli and Adelene were removed from the bus by police officers and taken to jail. This may remind you of a similar story that happened many years later. Claudette Colvin and Rosa Parks refused to give up their bus seats in 1956. Their protests were the beginning of the Montgomery bus boycott. Pauli Murray's protest was sixteen years earlier, and there were others who protested before Pauli and Adelene. Pauli lost the court case against the unjust bus segregation laws. A victory came years later.

Because of the success of the Montgomery bus boycott, segregation on buses was ruled against the law. Over time, African Americans could sit in any seat on a bus and travel from state to state freely. Very often, change is slow and happens over time. Pauli Murray did not change the laws

single-handedly. The voices and actions of protestors before and after Pauli, working together, brought about change. Together, they were all activists for justice.

8 ▪ Law School

Another seed was planted in Pauli's mind: Through studying the law, Pauli could better work toward equality for all people, protecting their rights and dignity. Pauli could be the voice for those who could not speak for themselves. In 1941 they began law school at Howard University in Washington, DC. Howard University was the first law school for African Americans in the United States. Pauli wanted very much to become a civil rights lawyer. Civil rights lawyers work to make sure all people have fair and equal treatment.

Thurgood Marshall, a civil rights activist who had also attended Howard University, wrote a letter of recommendation for Pauli. Later, Thurgood Marshall would become the first African American appointed to the Supreme Court. The Supreme Court is the highest court in the United States. The Court promises all American people equal justice according to the law.

Pauli was surprised by her treatment at Howard Law School. All the students attending Howard were African American. In Pauli's class were two women. By the end of the first year, Pauli was the only woman. Many men did not believe that women should be lawyers and did not take them seriously. Pauli felt this treatment was similar to Jim Crow laws that excluded people because of their race. Pauli named this unfair practice "Jane Crow." Jane Crow excluded women because of their race and gender. This made Pauli frustrated and angry. Anger, frustration, and unfair treatment did not present an obstacle but a challenge. Pauli stayed focused and would often say, "Don't get angry, get smart." That is exactly what they did.

While at Howard University, Pauli worked with other female students to protest segregation in restaurants in Washington, DC. When restaurants refused to serve Pauli and the other students, they sat quietly and politely at a table and read. When asked to leave, they remained seated and silent. The women did this day after day to call attention to the unfair practice of not serving African American customers. This action was known as "nonviolent protesting." It was an effective way to peacefully object to the restaurant's unfair rules. Not wanting to be involved with the protesters or have attention drawn to them, customers stopped coming to the restaurant. Over time, the restaurant began to lose business and eventually changed the laws to serve everyone.

Sit-ins, as they were called, were a popular form of nonviolent protest in the 1950s and 1960s. Once again, Pauli Murray was ahead of their time. This student group protested in 1944. The fight for civil rights did not begin with Pauli, though Pauli proudly joined the long line of activists, people who used their voices and actions to speak out against injustices. They demanded equal rights and dignity for all people in their time and those who came after.

Pauli worked hard and graduated from Howard Law School at the top of the class, gaining the respect of male classmates and continuing to fight not only against unjust laws based on race but also those based on gender. In 1966, Pauli helped form an organization to continue the fight for equal rights for all women. It is called NOW: National Organization for Women, and the group is still active today.

Pauli Murray wanted to learn and study more about law and applied to Harvard Law School, the oldest law school in the United States. Pauli was faced, again, with "Jane Crow." Harvard did not accept women. Pauli wrote to the law school in hopes they would change their mind but was unsuccessful. Instead, Pauli choose to attend the University of California, Berkeley, and earned a master's degree in law. Six years later, women were admitted to Harvard Law School.

Pauli Murray's law education did not end with a master's degree. In 1965, they received a third degree from Yale Law School. Yale is a top-ranked law school in the United States. There they received a JSD, a doctor of the science of law, the highest law degree. Pauli was the first in their family to receive such a degree from a major university. Pauli Murray was the first African American student to receive this degree from Yale.

9 ▪ Writing

Pauli Murray used the gift of writing throughout their life to capture all the passionate thoughts in their head. Writing provided a way to express fear, anger, loneliness, and even love. When Pauli was unable to physically protest, writing was an outlet to make their voice heard. Over the years Pauli wrote letters, poetry, magazine articles, and books in addition to their writings about the law.

When the women of the Methodist Church, who were against segregation, wanted to create a small pamphlet that would teach others about unfair segregation laws, Pauli Murray was hired for the job. Using their brilliant mind and gifted writing, they created a 746-page book. *States' Laws on Race and Color* was not only used by the women of the Methodist Church but colleges, law offices, and by Thurgood Marshall. He called the book "the bible" of the civil rights movement.

Pauli continued writing. They enjoyed capturing all the passionate thoughts in their head. Pauli Murray wrote several books about their family and their own life, along with poetry and writing about the law.

10 • Later Life

Throughout their life Pauli had many loves and passions. Among them were their love of family, teaching law, the continued fight for equality and human rights, and Irene Barlow, whom Pauli called their "silent partner." There was a spiritual bond between Irene and Pauli that connected their hearts. For sixteen years, Pauli and Irene loved and cared for one another. They did not speak or share their truth but simply lived it. Pauli believed that it was everyone's right to live freely.

For many years Pauli continued to do what they knew best, practicing and teaching law. Pauli taught law as far away as Africa and inspired many students who would also become lawyers. Pauli continued to give speeches, work toward equality and human rights, and maintained close relationships with women activists.

Then tragedy struck: Pauli's beloved Irene became ill and died. This was a turning point; Pauli began thinking of their own life. Pauli's work as an activist and lawyer had helped create change, but there was more to do. Pauli felt strongly that everything in life was pointing them in a new direction. Leaving work as a professor of law, civil rights studies, and women's studies at Brandeis University, a top university in Massachusetts, at the age of sixty-three, Pauli Murray decided to go back to school to become a priest in the Episcopal Church. Pauli was inspired by Martin Luther King Jr., the minister who had also worked for justice and peace. He dreamed of a peaceful world where people could work, play, and live together. Pauli also had dreamed and worked toward an undivided world. Two words Pauli often used guided her: liberation and reconciliation. Liberation means freeing people from the control of unfair laws and working for equal rights. Reconciliation means people coming together, working through a problem, and finding a solution that might work best. Reconciliation works best when people respect one another and share their ideas, thoughts, and fears. Pauli knew that the hard work of listening and working together toward justice and equality could change people's hearts and minds. This would create a more peaceful, less divided world.

With the encouragement of many friends, Pauli Murray entered seminary in 1973. Seminary is a school that prepares students to become ministers or priests.

As Pauli was growing up in the church, women were allowed to perform few jobs, such as Sunday school teacher, choir member or director, and altar guild (the altar guild are those who prepare the church for worship, cleaning the items used on the altar and putting them away after the service). At that time there were no female priests.

When Pauli entered seminary, there were very few women. Classes were made up of mostly white men and Pauli was the oldest student. With the same determination used to overcome other challenges in their life, Pauli studied and worked hard. They learned all they could about church history, their faith, and the traditions of the church.

Bishop Delaney, one of the first Black bishops in the Episcopal Church, recognized Pauli's gifts and potential. He had called Pauli a "child of destiny" when they were just eighteen years old. Almost fifty years later in January of 1977, Bishop Delaney's vision came true. Pauli Murray was ordained in the Episcopal Church. When someone is "ordained," it means that a person is made a priest during a special ceremony. Adding to those times when Pauli had been "first," Pauli became the first African American woman to become a priest in the church's history. Being a first, for Pauli, always meant opening the door for those who followed in their footsteps, making their path a little easier. The salt-and-pepper-haired, brown-skinned individual stood proudly and took their place in history.

In February of the same year Pauli traveled to Chapel Hill, North Carolina, to lead their first church service. It was the first

time a woman had led worship in an Episcopal Church in the state of North Carolina. To mark the celebration Pauli chose a special place for the service: Chapel of the Cross, the church where their enslaved grandmother had been baptized. Life's winding path that once opened before Pauli had led to this day.

Pauli served as priest in several churches in three states. They retired at the age of seventy-two and continued to visit and care for the sick.

11 ▪ Fearfully and Wonderfully Made

On July 1, 1985, Pauli Murray reached the end of their long journey. They died in Pittsburgh, Pennsylvania, of cancer.

Who knew young Anna Pauline Murray would grow up and change the world? Pauli had gone from the world of Jim Crow laws to a world that was more free of legal segregation. They learned, from a young age, the importance of family, faith, hard work, and study. As a young child, Pauli learned to speak out and protest things they disliked. They knew and accepted that they were different—an individual, smart and outspoken. Pauli did not fit neatly into what people thought they should be. They chose not to be confined by race, gender, or age. Walking into a room, people knew Pauli was someone special. Small in body but with a big personality, they were proud and held their head high. Pauli Murray was a dedicated lawyer, activist, poet, writer, and priest. Always fighting against unfair laws based on race and gender, Pauli's legacy and gift is the example of an authentic life well lived.

In July of 2012 Pauli Murray was chosen to be commemorated by the Episcopal Church. Listed on the official calendar for the Episcopal Church, Pauli is recognized as the first African American priest of their gender and for their life's work for justice and freedom. Pauli's life and work will continue to inspire and bring hope for many generations to come. Courageously, Pauli Murray lived the hopes and dreams of their ancestors.

Upon their death Pauli Murray left a large collection of pictures, letters, diaries, speeches, and writings. Among the writing are words that continue to inspire:

> When my brothers try to draw a circle to exclude me, I shall draw a larger circle to include them. Where they speak out for the privileges of a puny group, I shall shout for the rights of all mankind.
>
> —Dr. Pauli Murray

Glossary

Reader: This glossary has some words you may not be familiar with. Ask a relative or teacher if you still have questions. Some words may have more than one meaning. The definitions below describe the usage of these words as presented in this book.

Civil rights movement. The modern civil rights movement began in the mid-1950s. People who believed in racial equality and social justice participated in a series of actions, marches, sit-ins, and protests to end discrimination and racial segregation. These events ended with the creation of new laws.

Commemorate. To respectfully remember a person's life and work.

Discrimination. To treat a person or a group of people differently or unfairly because of their race or gender.

Gender.[1] There are many ways to define gender. The concept of gender has evolved since the early 1900s when Pauli was

---

1. You may choose to discuss the idea of gender with an adult whose opinion you respect.

born. Fear, lack of understanding, and lack of acceptance limited people's thinking. How a person was born biologically determined whether they were male or female. Today the language and understanding is more widely accepted and inclusive.

Integrate. To bring together, equally, different races of people.

Lifelong. A quality or trait that lasts throughout a person's life.

Prejudice. To judge a person or group based on information that is not true.

Pronoun. A word used to refer to a person, other than their name, that they would feel comfortable with and respond to. She/her, they/them, and he/him are examples of pronouns.

Psalm. A special poem or song used in a church service or as a prayer. The Bible contains a book of psalms.

Race. A group of people who share physical traits, a common history, and culture.

Segregation. To keep people apart from one another because of race or religion. For many years segregation was enforced by laws.

Sit-in. A form of nonviolent protest where a person or group sits in a space and refuses to move. The sitting happens over time to call attention to an unfair rule or law.

Timeline

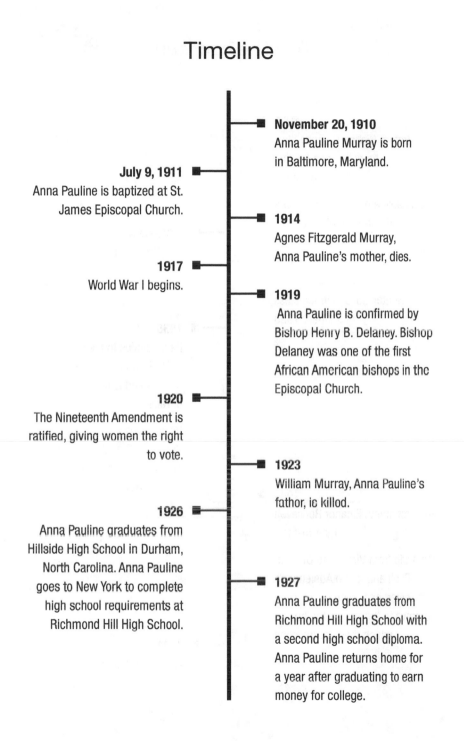

November 20, 1910
Anna Pauline Murray is born in Baltimore, Maryland.

July 9, 1911
Anna Pauline is baptized at St. James Episcopal Church.

1914
Agnes Fitzgerald Murray, Anna Pauline's mother, dies.

1917
World War I begins.

1919
Anna Pauline is confirmed by Bishop Henry B. Delaney. Bishop Delaney was one of the first African American bishops in the Episcopal Church.

1920
The Nineteenth Amendment is ratified, giving women the right to vote.

1923
William Murray, Anna Pauline's father, is killed.

1926
Anna Pauline graduates from Hillside High School in Durham, North Carolina. Anna Pauline goes to New York to complete high school requirements at Richmond Hill High School.

1927
Anna Pauline graduates from Richmond Hill High School with a second high school diploma. Anna Pauline returns home for a year after graduating to earn money for college.

Timeline *continued*

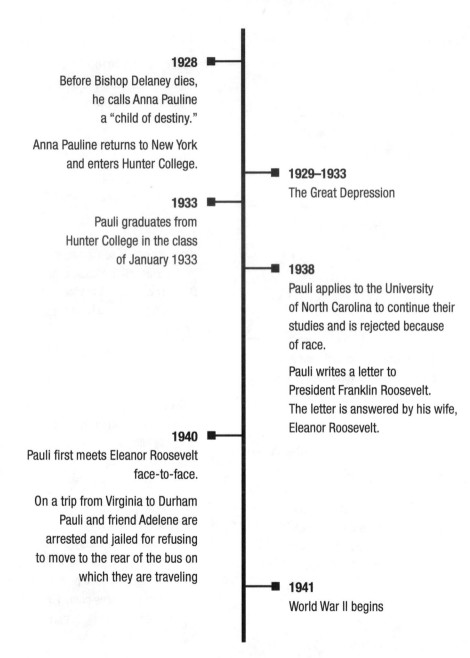

1928

Before Bishop Delaney dies,
he calls Anna Pauline
a "child of destiny."

Anna Pauline returns to New York
and enters Hunter College.

1929–1933

The Great Depression

1933

Pauli graduates from
Hunter College in the class
of January 1933

1938

Pauli applies to the University
of North Carolina to continue their
studies and is rejected because
of race.

Pauli writes a letter to
President Franklin Roosevelt.
The letter is answered by his wife,
Eleanor Roosevelt.

1940

Pauli first meets Eleanor Roosevelt
face-to-face.

On a trip from Virginia to Durham
Pauli and friend Adelene are
arrested and jailed for refusing
to move to the rear of the bus on
which they are traveling

1941

World War II begins

Timeline *continued*

1941
Pauli enters law school at Howard University. Pauli is one of two women in the class and begins to feel the difference in treatment, labeling it "Jane Crow."

1944
Pauli graduates at the top of the law school class. Pauli applies to Harvard Law School and is rejected because of gender.

1945
Pauli attends the University of California Law School at Berkeley for postgraduate studies.

Pauli passes the California Bar Exam.

1946
California appoints its first African American deputy attorney general.

1950
Pauli publishes *States' Laws on Race and Color.* Thurgood Marshall calls it the civil rights bible.

1954
Brown vs. Board of Education: "separate but equal" is ruled unconstitutional.

1955
Montgomery Bus Boycott.

Vietnam War begins.

Timeline *continued*

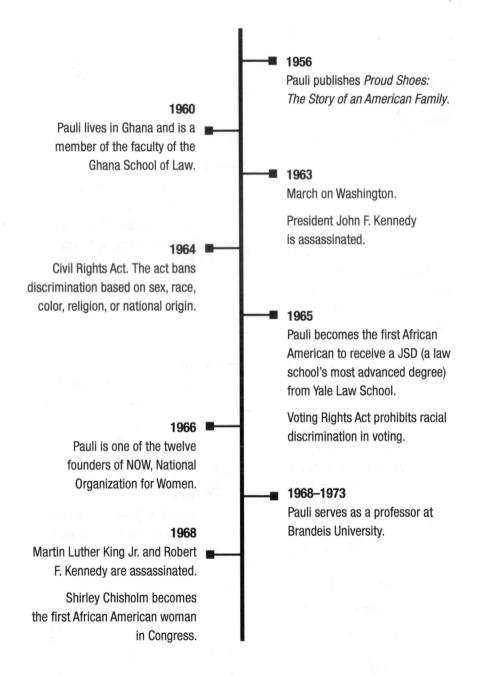

1956
Pauli publishes *Proud Shoes: The Story of an American Family.*

1960
Pauli lives in Ghana and is a member of the faculty of the Ghana School of Law.

1963
March on Washington.

President John F. Kennedy is assassinated.

1964
Civil Rights Act. The act bans discrimination based on sex, race, color, religion, or national origin.

1965
Pauli becomes the first African American to receive a JSD (a law school's most advanced degree) from Yale Law School.

Voting Rights Act prohibits racial discrimination in voting.

1966
Pauli is one of the twelve founders of NOW, National Organization for Women.

1968–1973
Pauli serves as a professor at Brandeis University.

1968
Martin Luther King Jr. and Robert F. Kennedy are assassinated.

Shirley Chisholm becomes the first African American woman in Congress.

Timeline *continued*

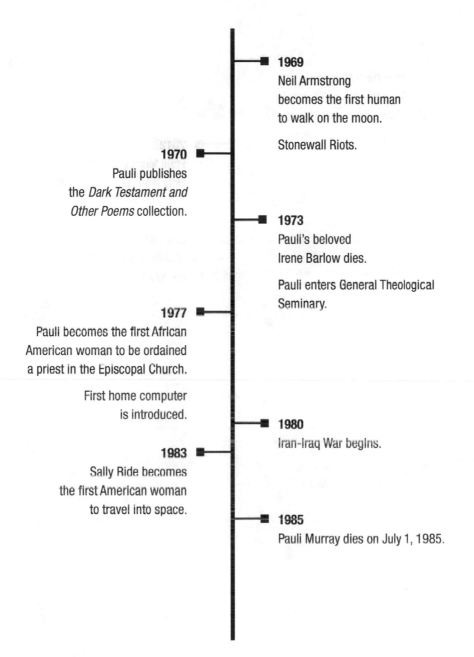

1969
Neil Armstrong
becomes the first human
to walk on the moon.

Stonewall Riots.

1970
Pauli publishes
the *Dark Testament and
Other Poems* collection.

1973
Pauli's beloved
Irene Barlow dies.

Pauli enters General Theological
Seminary.

1977
Pauli becomes the first African
American woman to be ordained
a priest in the Episcopal Church.

First home computer
is introduced.

1980
Iran-Iraq War begins.

1983
Sally Ride becomes
the first American woman
to travel into space.

1985
Pauli Murray dies on July 1, 1985.

Timeline *continued*

1987 ◼

After Pauli Murray's death, *Song in a Weary Throat: An American Pilgrimage*, Murray's autobiography, is published.

◼ **2012**

Pauli Murray is added to *Holy Women, Holy Men*, an official volume for the Episcopal Church commemorating those of significance on the date of their death. Pauli is celebrated on July 1.

About the Author and Illustrator

Deborah Nelson Linck is a writer and retired elementary educator. She is the founder and curator of The Hands-On Black History Museum where she educates communities about the importance of Black History. Deborah lives in St. Louis, Missouri.

Angela Corbin is a freelance illustrator based in Maryland. She has a background in children's books, comics, and character design.

CPSIA information can be obtained
at www.ICGtesting.com
Printed in the USA
JSHW021719041222
34171JS00003B/3